Computer
Error

Linda Strachan

Illustrated by Tony Albers

Rigby

Contents

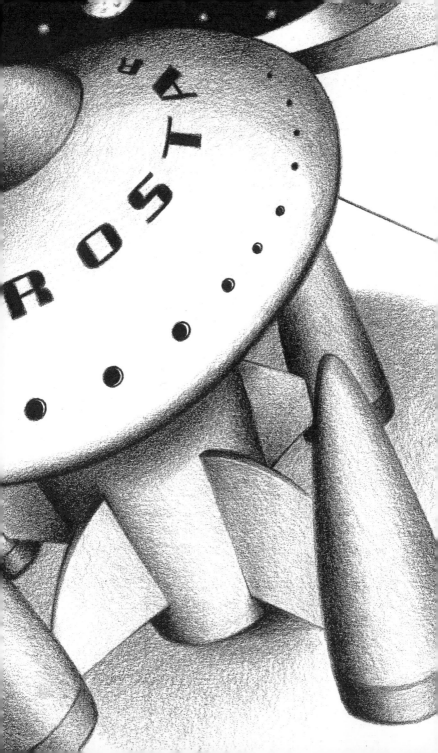

CHAPTER ONE

The *Rostar*

FREYA and her little brother, Chas, couldn't believe their luck. The spaceship that was taking them home for the holidays was the newest ship in the Galactic Fleet.

"Wait until I tell them I was on the *Rostar*. The kids at school will be green with envy!" Freya told Chas as they boarded the ship at the space dock.

Chas looked up at the shiny new ship. He was a little frightened, so he

hid behind Freya as they went into the elevator. But Freya didn't notice.

She was used to Chas being shy when they went to new places. She knew he didn't like meeting people, so she usually did most of the talking.

"See that, Chas?" Freya was so excited she was almost jumping up and down. "That's the new voice-operated system. They can tell who we are just by listening to us!"

Chas shivered. He didn't like that idea at all. "W-w-will they let us in, Freya?" he asked. His speech always got worse when he was scared.

"Of course they will! Freya and Chas Roberts requesting permission to come on board the *Rostar*," she said in a proud voice.

"Welcome to the *Rostar*, Freya and Chas. This is Captain Hope. Please come on board."

The elevator started to move, and when the doors opened again, the captain was waiting to meet them. On the way to their cabin, she promised them a tour of the ship.

Freya couldn't wait. She knew that the *Rostar* was run by the newest and smartest computer ever to be installed in a spaceship.

She had all sorts of questions she wanted to ask. The captain told them to come to the passengers' dining room when they were ready.

When Freya and Chas left their cabin a little while later, Freya saw some of the other passengers coming down the corridor. Suddenly, a red light swept from their shoulders to the tops of their heads.

Then the strangest thing happened. The passengers just disappeared! Freya couldn't believe her eyes.

CHAPTER TWO

A Mystery

WHEN CHAS told her he hadn't seen anything, Freya began to wonder if she had imagined it.

They went off to find the passengers' dining room. It was a large room with lots of tables and chairs. An enormous window looked out into space. A lot of passengers were sitting at the tables, eating and drinking.

One of the crew, Ensign Kora, came over to speak to them. She was going to take them on their tour of the ship.

"Would you like something to drink first?" Kora asked.

"Yes, please!" Freya said, staring out the window.

"How about you, Chas?" Kora asked him. Chas just looked up at her.

"He'd like one, too, Kora," Freya said, putting an arm around her little brother. "He's a bit shy," she explained.

"Are there any other kids on board the ship?" Freya asked as she sipped her drink.

"No, Freya." Kora shook her head. "Not on this trip. This is our first long trip, and most of the passengers are scientists."

Kora took them on a tour of the ship. As they were leaving the ship's medical center, Freya turned back to have a last look. She saw the red light again. It seemed to pass just above her. It passed across the heads of the doctor and his two assistants. Then, just as before, they all disappeared.

Freya turned and yelled at Kora to come quickly. Kora and Chas came running back, and they looked in the door to where Freya was pointing.

"Look!" she said. Her eyes were wide with shock. "It's happened again. They've disappeared! The doctor! Everyone! They just disappeared!"

Kora listened as Freya told her how she had seen the red light and then everyone disappeared. "It happened before, just outside our cabin. I told Chas." She turned to Chas. "I told you, didn't I?"

Chas nodded. "She did, Kora."

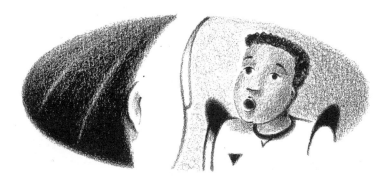

Kora looked thoughtful for a moment. "It sounds like a transporter beam," she said slowly. "I'll check with the control room. But they only transport the doctor out of here like that in an emergency."

Kora pressed a button on her sleeve and spoke to the control room.

"Control, has the doctor been transported out of the medical center in the last few minutes?"

"No, Ensign Kora. There have been no transports in that area of the ship."

"Can you tell me where the doctor is at the moment?"

There was a pause. When the control officer spoke again, he sounded puzzled. "The doctor does not seem to be on board."

CHAPTER THREE

Computer Error

"I THINK WE should go back to the dining room," Kora said. She looked worried.

"What's happening?" Freya asked.

Kora flashed a quick smile. "I'm sure it's nothing, Freya."

They went back to the dining room, but just as the door slid open, Freya saw the red light sweep across the room. Just like before, all the people disappeared.

Kora pressed the button on her sleeve. "Control! Control! The passengers in the dining room have just been transported. Just like the doctor! They're gone!"

"This is Captain Hope. Where are Freya and Chas Roberts?"

"They're here with me, Captain," said Kora, out of breath.

Freya felt Chas grab her arm. He was shaking.

"Wh-what's going on, Freya?" he asked.

"It will be okay, Chas. I'll take care of you." Freya put her arm around him. But inside she was feeling scared, too.

Kora turned to Freya and Chas. "The captain says we all have to go to the control room. She wants everyone who is left on the ship to meet there."

Freya and Chas followed Kora through the ship. A voice sounded all over the ship.

"This is the captain. All passengers and crew are to report to the control room immediately. This is not a drill!"

When they arrived at the control room, it was full of people. They were all talking at once and asking questions. Freya was listening to the

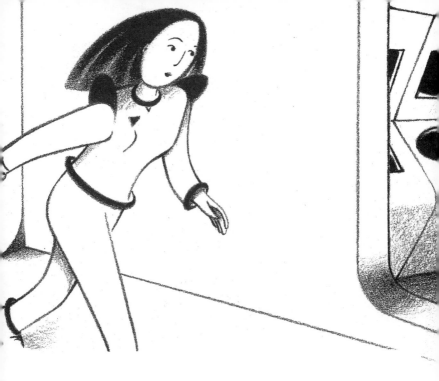

captain as she talked to Kora. She heard the captain asking Kora what she had seen.

"It sounds like the computer has started transporting everyone off the ship. The problem is, where do they end up?" Freya thought the captain looked really worried, and she wondered where the captain thought the computer was sending everyone.

One of the crew members came over. "There seems to be over sixty people missing, Captain."

"It must be the sensors," the captain was saying.

Suddenly, Freya saw something that made her legs turn to water. "Look!" she said.

The captain looked over to where Freya was pointing. She saw the red light sweep across one end of the room. It swept across the heads of the people standing there. A moment later, they all disappeared.

The light was starting to pass over the rest of the people in the room. Freya bent down to hug Chas. She knew he would be even more scared than she was.

But when she looked up, they were alone in the control room!

CHAPTER FOUR

All Alone

CHAS STARED at the empty room. There were tears in his eyes.

"Wh-wh-where has everyone gone, Freya?" he asked. His voice was shaking.

Freya swallowed and coughed before she could speak. She couldn't believe it. Everyone else had gone. They were all alone on the ship. Freya could hear Chas sniffing as he tried not to cry.

She had to be strong for Chas. He was her little brother, and now she was the only one who could take care of him.

"It'll be okay, Chas," she said, putting on a brave smile. "I think the captain said something about sensors. That must be what the red light was!"

"Did it miss us because we're too small?" Chas asked her.

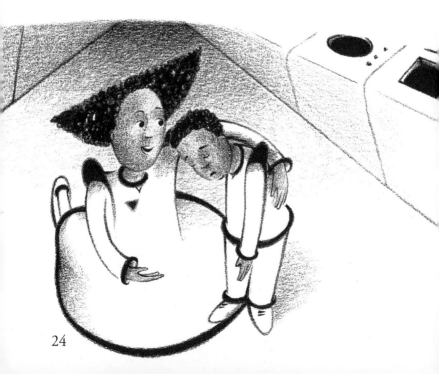

Freya looked at her little brother for a moment. She had been leaning down to hug him when the red light swept across the room. Could Chas be right? Maybe that was why they were left on the *Rostar* when everyone else was transported off the ship.

"That was very smart, Chas!" she said, giving him a hug. Freya looked around the control room. What would she do now?

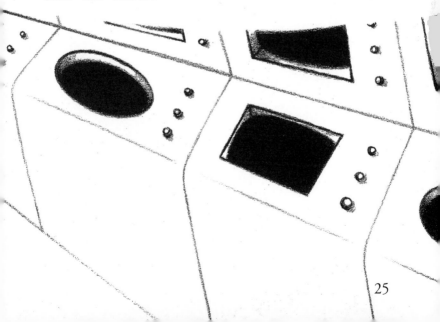

Suddenly she saw the red light begin to sweep the room again.

"Get down, Chas!" she yelled, pulling him down behind a desk.

The red light was coming from a panel on the wall. Freya had seen these all over the ship. She wasn't very tall, and the panels were all just higher than her head.

"Can you see where the light is coming from, Chas?" She pointed to the panel.

Chas followed her finger and nodded when he saw the panel.

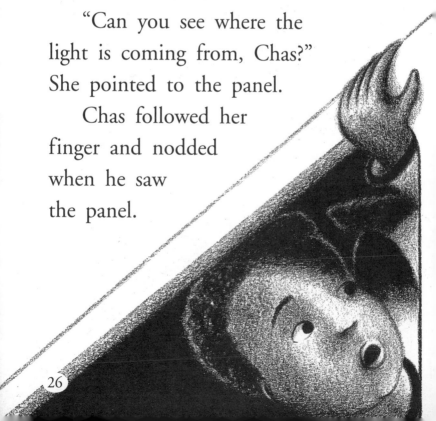

"We can't let the light touch us. So you have to stay low when we pass one of those panels."

Chas looked up at her. His eyes were wide with fear.

"Don't worry, Chas," she said, sounding more sure than she felt. "We'll be all right!"

The door was standing open just behind them. "Let's get out of here," she said.

Freya crawled out of the room, tugging Chas behind her. She pulled him to his feet behind the door and checked the walls for sensor panels.

"We have to find someplace safe," Freya whispered to Chas. "Then we can decide what to do."

CHAPTER FIVE

Emergency

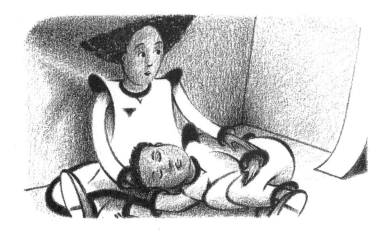

A FEW hours later, Freya and Chas were sitting in the corner of a small room. It was the only room that didn't have any sensors in it. Chas had fallen asleep, and Freya was trying to think of what they could do next.

A voice sounded through the empty ship. It was very loud, and it scared Freya.

"Freya! Chas! Can you hear me? This is Captain Hope. All the passengers from the ship have been transported safely to the planet Adnile. We found out what happened—the new computer broke down, and we think you weren't tall enough for the sensors to find you."

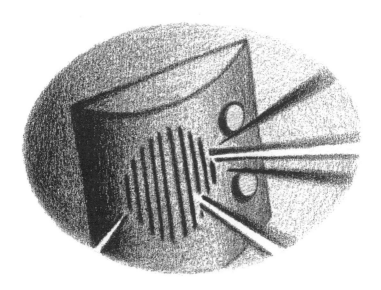

Chas woke up and smiled when he heard that.

"It is very important for the two of you to stay on the ship. You can't let the sensors touch you. The computer is very clever and it'll soon discover that you're on the ship. It will change the sensors and they will flash closer to the ground."

Freya frowned. If everyone else was transported to another planet, why shouldn't she and Chas let the computer send them down, too? The next thing the captain said changed her mind.

"You can't let the computer send you to the new planet. The ship is heading toward the biggest city on the planet Adnile. If we can't shut down the computer, we will never be able to stop the ship from crashing into the city."

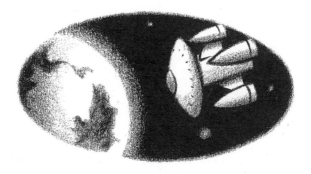

CHAPTER SIX

Run, Chas!

FREYA WAS suddenly scared. The ship was going to crash, and she and Chas couldn't get off it.

The captain began to speak again. "I need you to be very brave, Freya. You have to get into the computer room without letting the sensors find you. You'll find a green panel marked SENSORS. You must press that panel to switch off the sensors. Then I can come back from planet Adnile using a transport sensor and stop the ship from crashing."

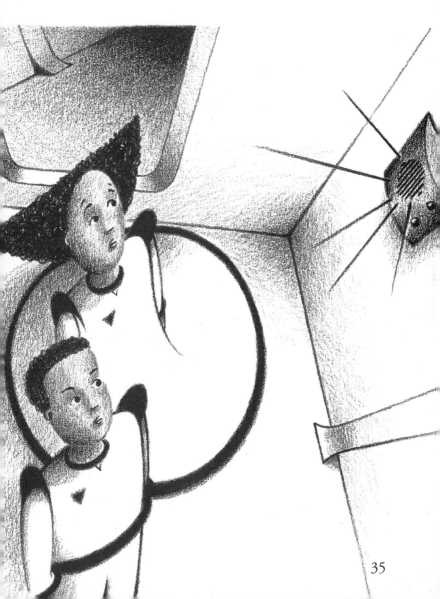

Freya was still scared. She had to take care of Chas, but now she had to save the ship, too. She didn't think she could do it. She sat hugging her knees.

Chas got up and pulled her sleeve. "We have to go, Freya," he said. He rubbed his eyes to make sure he was awake. "The captain said we had to!"

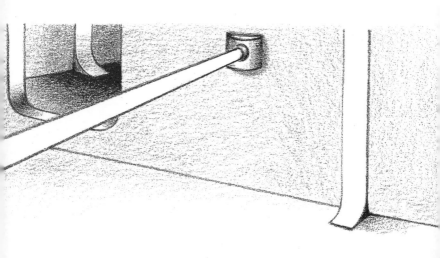

Freya looked at her little brother. She was really proud of him. She knew he was scared, too.

Freya remembered that the computer room was not too far from where they were. She took Chas by the hand, and they crept along the corridor toward the computer room. As they passed, the red light swept the corridor behind them.

"Run, Chas!" she yelled, and they both ran as fast as they could toward the next door. It was the computer room. Freya carefully pushed the pad that made the door open. The door slid open and Freya looked inside.

"There are lots of panels in there, Freya," Chas whispered. Freya started counting the sensor panels. There were ten of them on the walls of the room and one more on the ceiling.

"Can you see the green panel, Chas?" she asked him.

Chas was crawling on the floor just inside the room. He spotted the green panel marked SENSORS. Then he saw a red light come toward him, and he hurled himself out of the room.

"I saw it, Freya!" he said. "It's on the back wall."

Freya took a deep breath. She knew she had to get in there before the sensors touched her.

CHAPTER SEVEN

Rescue

"**Y**OU STAY HERE, Chas, and stay low!" She stopped to smile at Chas and then ran across the room as fast as she could.

It seemed to take forever to get to the other end of the room. She could see the red sensor light starting to sweep across the room. She ran faster and faster.

Just as she reached the far wall, she heard Chas cry out. "I'll stop it, Freya!" he shouted.

Freya spun around.

"Chas! No!" she yelled, but it was too late. He had been standing in the room, and the sensor had found him. She watched, horrified, as he disappeared.

Another red sensor light was cross-
ing the room toward her. Freya spun
around and reached for the green
panel. She found it and pressed it as
hard as she could. She hoped she'd be
in time, but the red light had started
to cross her foot ...

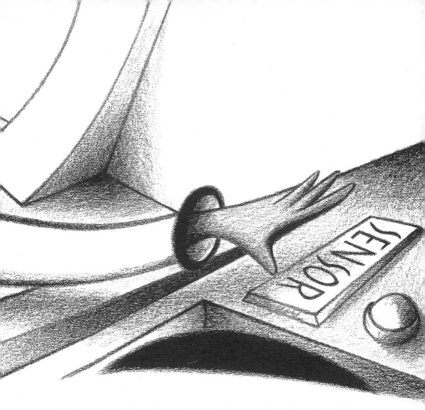

Suddenly the light vanished. Freya realized that she'd done it. She had switched off the sensors!

She stood there, not knowing what to do next. Then she heard the captain's voice.

"Good job, Freya. Come to the control room and I'll show you how we stopped the ship from crashing."

Freya ran through the ship to the control room. When she got there, it was full of people. They all cheered when she came in, but Freya was looking for her brother.

"Well done, Freya," said the captain. "Once you turned off the sensors, I could use the Adnile transporter beam to bring us back to the ship. And look who came back from the planet with us!"

Standing next to the captain was Chas. "We did it, Freya!" he said with a grin.

"Yes, Chas, we did!"